Sand!

Written by Claire Llewellyn
Illustrated by Lauren Beard

WAYLAND

There is sand on
my hands.

There is sand on my legs.

There is sand on
my towel.

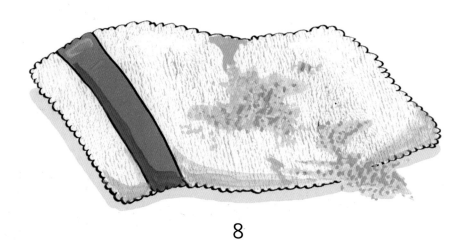

There is sand on
my face.

There is sand on
my banana.

There is sand on
my bottom.

There is sand on
my teddy.

There is sand on
my feet.

21

Guiding a First Read
Sand!

It is important to talk through the book with the child before they attempt to read it alone. This will build confidence and enable the child to tackle the first read without feeling overwhelmed. Look at the pictures together, read the book title, and pick out words of interest and the high frequency words for discussion.

The high frequency words in this title are:
is   my   on

1. Talking through the book

It is time to go home from the beach, but there is sand everywhere.

> **Let's read the title: Sand!**
> **Turn to page 4. Let's have a look at the picture. The girl says, "There is sand on my...?" Yes, hands.**
>
> **Now turn to page 6. What does she say on this page?**

Continue to read the book, with the child looking at the illustrations, for example on page 14:

> **Yes, there is sand on her bum, but this page says bottom.**
> **And on page 20 she's all clean, and she says, "No more sand!"**

2. A first reading of the book

Ask the child to read the book independently and point carefully underneath each word (tracking), while thinking about the story.

Work with the child, prompting them and praising their careful tracking, attempts to correct themselves and their knowledge of letters and sounds:

> **How did you know that says teddy?**
> **Yes, it's a teddy in the picture and**
> **the word starts with 't'.**

3. Follow-up activities

- Select a high frequency word, as listed on p22, and ask the child to find it throughout the book. Discuss the shape of the letters and the letter sounds.

- To memorise the word, ask the child to write it in the air, then write it repeatedly on a whiteboard or on paper, leaving a space between each attempt.

- Alternate writing the new word starting with a capital letter, and then with a lower-case letter.

4. Encourage

- Rereading of the book many times.

- Drawing a picture based on the story.

- Writing a sentence using the practised word.

START READING is a series of highly enjoyable books for beginner readers. **The books have been carefully graded to match the Book Bands widely used in schools.** This enables readers to be sure they choose books that match their own reading ability.

Look out for the Band colour on the book in our Start Reading logo.

The Bands are:

Pink Band 1A and 1B

Red Band 2

Yellow Band 3

Blue Band 4

Green Band 5

Orange Band 6

Turquoise Band 7

Purple Band 8

Gold Band 9

START READING books can be read independently or shared with an adult. They promote the enjoyment of reading through satisfying stories supported by fun illustrations.

Claire Llewellyn has written many books for children. Some of them are about real things like animals and the Moon, others are storybooks. Claire has two children, but they are getting too big for stories like this one. She hopes you will enjoy reading her stories instead.

Lauren Beard was born in Bolton in 1984. She graduated from Loughborough University in 2006. That same year she came runner up in the Macmillan children's book prize. Since graduating she has had numerous books published and now works in a studio in Manchester.